The Estate Appraiser

a story about antiques, art and vintage murder

Lesann Berry

Isinglass Press
SILVERLAKE, WASHINGTON

Isinglass Press
PO Box 1731
Castle Rock, WA 98611
www.isinglasspress.com

Publisher's Note: This is a work of fiction. Names, characters, places, and incidents are a product of the author's imagination. Locales and public names are sometimes used for atmospheric purposes. Any resemblance to actual people, living or dead, or to businesses, companies, events, institutions, or locales is completely coincidental.

Cover Design by Melody Simmons at www. ebookindiecovers.com
Interior Design by www.BookDesignTemplates.com

Ordering Information:
Quantity sales. Special discounts are available on quantity purchases by corporations, associations, and others. For details, contact the "Special Sales Department" at the address above.

The Estate Appraiser/ Lesann Berry. -- 1st ed.
ISBN 978-1-939316-05-9

For those who got surprised by graduation.

School may be over but education continues.

–ANONYMOUS

CHAPTER ONE

The Debate

Some people just know what they're going to be when they grow up. You probably remember the kind of person I'm talking about, those weird kids who announce their desire to become biologists, psychologists, or school counselors when what they should be wondering is which color of sweatshirt to pack for summer camp. I was not one of those kids. I fell more into the what-do-you-mean-childhood-doesn't-last-forever crowd. High school graduation forced the issue and rather than search for gainful employment, I headed straight for the nearest university. My parents were thrilled, once the shock wore off. The excitement lasted until my junior year when I phoned one evening and announced plans to major in art history.

On my visit home the following weekend, Dad studied me with a vague expression of alarm. His wire-rimmed glasses, reflecting light from the lamp beside his chair, flashed as he shook his head and struggled to make sense of my decision. "Art is wonderful Lydia, but what about something useful, like an accounting degree?"

"The Humanities are important, Dad. Art history has value." I countered, prepared to argue.

My father stared at me, his lips twisted in a doubtful smile. I was just happy to finish my general education requirements and find a field interesting enough to keep me from dropping out of school. Also there was no advanced math requirement.

While Dad tried to talk sense to me, Mom went to the kitchen and started mixing a batch of cookies. Mom bakes for stress relief. I didn't worry about losing my back-up. In time, I knew she'd take my side because she harbored a love for all things antique and the crossover to art was natural. Their house was stuffed with refinished Victorian furniture and restored vintage junk Mom had rescued from rummage sales and second-hand boutiques all over the New England countryside.

From that weekend on, Dad never stopped trying to encourage me to seek out a practical way to apply my new knowledge. Every visit home for a holiday was another skirmish in the battle for my career path. Over Thanksgiving turducken he suggested I apply for on-the-job training at one of the multinational insurance companies whose skyscrapers speared the skyline. By the time Easter rolled around he'd hatched a new plan. He'd pulled some strings inside the old-guy network and lined up a trial period for me to work-at-home processing adjustment claims for an insurance firm and cold-calling policy holders to upsell company products.

I shuddered at the mere thought.

"I think your internship at the Museum of Modern Art is fabulous, Lydia, but it doesn't offer a salary. The position with Ameri-Justis provides income. Just think about it, okay?"

Dad was subtle but insistent.

Volunteer hours at the museum consumed my weekends during the spring. I learned about how collections are amassed – in the art world it really does matter who you know. The organizational systems for storing and displaying art are far more complicated than I ever guessed. So much thought and planning goes into deciding how to arrange pieces in relation to one another. I loved every minute of the process. The curatorial staff was fun. The atmosphere was exciting.

A paycheck would have made it perfect.

Mom mailed me boxes of baked goods. Inside, she always tucked a hand-written note of encouragement. Guess which side of my family harbors a rebellious strain?

I called Dad on Father's Day and patiently listened as he suggested I contact one of his golf cronies at some financial institution across the river. "Call Billy and tell him you're available." After a pause, as he waited for me to emit a mumble of conscientious dissent, he pushed forward with a dose of parental guilt. "Really, honey, I just want what's best for your future. Billy is one of my oldest clients and he said he'd be happy to offer you an entry level position."

As if I'd even contemplate commuting *out* of town. "That's a super idea, Dad, and it's a really generous opportunity. Truly. Please give my regards to Billy, but as you know, I'm not interested in finance. You're the one who likes numbers. Besides, I've signed up for a summer internship at the MOMA."

I went home for the long Fourth of July weekend. Dad regaled me with statistics about the relative merit of income earned and the long-term value of an education with practical skills. Obviously, the path I trod was headed straight to financial ruin.

"Do you remember Emily Branswittel, Clancy and June's daughter?"

I nodded. Emily had been a senior the year I'd started high school.

"She works as a phlebotomist at Mercy Hospital in Newark and makes a solid living. You could do the same." He smiled at me, his eyes crinkling at the edges of his glasses, as he waited for my reaction.

The debate had taken on a game-like quality. I rallied immediately. "I suppose. Somehow working with biohazards doesn't have the same appeal for me as it must for Emily. Instead, I've signed up to be a trainee at the Avenue Art Gallery in Chelsea. Starting in September, I'll be rubbing shoulders with the rich and famous, getting firsthand experience in the high-end market of buying and selling art treasures among the demimonde."

Dad laughed so hard he spilled his iced tea.

And that was the pattern we settled into over the next year. For the most part, I ignored Dad's suggestions, dismissing his concerns until graduation came and went. The day I pulled the letter from the student loan corporation out of my mailbox, my bubble burst. The dollar amount displayed in the money-owed column produced a wail of disbelief. No way could I have spent that much acquiring a bachelor's degree. Wrong. A dozen pleading phone calls to the loan representative confirmed the number was not a typo. I had a six month grace period before the repayment schedule kicked in. The clock was ticking.

CHAPTER TWO

Reality Check

My half-hearted idea of enrolling in graduate school evapo-
rated like a puff of steam. I needed income. Fast. Like immediately.

Dad's words echoing in my ears, I sat down and added up
my living expenses. Sandwiched somewhere between the
neighborhood of "holy crow" and "goose egg zilch" sat my

income. Even with my rudimentary mathematical skills, I knew I was in trouble. Fortunately, I'd paid the lease on my apartment through August. My checking account contained enough cash to tide me over until the end of summer, but only if I practiced excessive frugality. I would have to invite myself to dinner at the neighbors' at least once a week. If I wasn't employed by the time September rolled in, the cupboard would be bare.

Any thought of moving home got a swift rejection. Few opportunities existed in the rural burg where Mom and Dad lived. While I appreciated their semi-retired lifestyle, I didn't want to rusticate with them. I loved the city. The clanking and stench, the outrageous lights and insane cost of living, filled me with energy. I briefly considered moving to a cheaper apartment but the savings didn't balance out the possibility of being mugged every time I stepped outside. My neighborhood offered the rare combination of lower rents and relatively safe streets, owing primarily to the community efforts of the local Polish families who patrolled the area after dark.

Sitting in front of my battered laptop, I scanned e-mails. I'd sent out more than two dozen résumés in the last week, but despite my affirmations about the importance of art and history to my father, fate had proved him correct yet again. Nobody wanted an employee with my degree. The department faculty had talked up numerous job positions, places where majors like me could apply our specialized knowledge. Unfortunately, I found few openings. Like zero.

I'd already applied to every museum position that offered an actual salary. After a solid week spent tweaking my resume and experience to fit the paid positions, I reshuffled and applied to the handful of paid internships that only the largest museum complexes could afford to offer. Competition was fierce. Willing to get my foot in the door using any access, I applied for positions in the museum gift shops and cafes. A review of the educational requirements, expected skills and abilities, and starting pay-scale for a janitorial position appealed to my new practicality. I submitted my application there too.

I clicked the send and receive button: nothing new in the queue.

I phoned the galley in Chelsea where I'd interned, a euphemistic term for working-the-volunteer-like-a-dog. Simon, the gallery manager answered the phone and I point-blank asked for a job.

"Well of course we'd love to have you back, Lydia. I can offer you thirty hours a week in the evenings."

I felt warm fuzzies for Simon. "How much does it pay?" He snorted and my heart sank. "I can't afford to work for free." I made no effort to hide the whine in my tone.

"You gotta pay your dues in this business, dearie."

"I gotta pay my student loans."

He laughed again, made kissing noises and hung up.

I couldn't work up any resentment. Simon might be a class-A-jerk, but I was one of the few people who knew he had an advanced degree in mathematics and couldn't find a job in his chosen field. Knowing he sympathized, somewhere deep inside, I redialed. I'd counted eight rings before Simon picked up the receiver.

"Nothing doing, darling. I didn't find a paying position in the last sixty seconds." He paused and let the silence stretch out for a beat. "Unless, that is, you can offer me something special?"

The suggestive tone turned the innocuous phrase into an innuendo-laden minefield. I wracked my brain for a clever riposte. Simon was blatantly open about his sexuality so I knew he wasn't interested in me, at least not physically.

"Find your own boy-toys, you trollop."

He snickered. "Well then, what good are you to me?"

"I'm desperate. I need advice. How do I find a job in this godforsaken city?"

Simon's amusement trickled into my ear. I heard his nimble fingers tapping on the keyboard, could picture him sitting behind the glass and chrome counter, his back to the garishly painted monstrous canvas mounted to the wall behind him. There was a pause in his typing and then a sharp staccato of keystrokes.

"Are you gaming while I'm having a life crisis?"

He grunted an affirmative.

"Geek. I'm appealing to your better side, Simon. You could at least pretend to listen."

Another clatter of hard-keying punctuated his chortle. "Okay, my raven-haired beauty, here's the secret to employment in New York –"

I hunched my shoulders and pressed the phone tighter to my ear.

"Network, my dear. Pimp yourself to all and sundry."

"I'm doing that right now," I complained.

"I'm worthless to you, but at least you're on the right track. He smacked a kiss in my ear and slammed down the receiver.

I dropped the cordless phone back into the cradle and slumped in my desk chair. I'd already burned through my connections in the art community and put the word out through my patchwork of professional relationships. Everyone I'd graduated with was in the same boat. We were all scrambling for work, preferably in a position related to our field. I needed to focus on new resources. Who else could I mine for assistance?

A sudden inspiration struck.

I rummaged through my old course files until I latched on to the syllabus from a class I'd taken the previous autumn. The instructor, a middle-aged woman named Professor Baumgarten had once mentioned how she subsidized her teaching income by processing estates. I pounced on her e-mail address, typed a quick message, and pressed send. Maybe my desperate tone would draw sympathy.

I dutifully applied for three more jobs, all for which I lacked the appropriate experience and qualifications, but what the hell. Nothing ventured, nothing gained, right? I'd abandoned Craigslist as a viable option after my e-mail became jammed with sex-for-hire solicitations. All I'd done was post a job-wanted notice, but apparently I wasn't specific enough in detailing my terms of employment. The help-wanted column of the local daily took most of an hour to scan since I considered every listing. Desperate enough to work the counter at a deli, the only positions still available was for a receptionist at a daycare center or a delivery driver at a flower shop. Tiny Tykes wanted eighteen units of child development coursework. Scratch that idea. The florist specified someone with a car. Strike three. The day began to take on a depressing shape.

I contemplated calling my dad and confessing, saying to him, "You were right. Can I borrow a few bucks?" The thought caused a shudder. My parents had subsidized my expenses while I found my academic footing. Without them, I'd owe twice as much to the student loan people. Throwing Dad's good advice back in his face seemed bad form. He'd never gloat, just look at me over the tops of his glasses and appear concerned. I couldn't stand the thought. I glanced across the studio apartment to the crumpled pile of bedding near the window. I'd made my bed, now I just wanted to lay in it for a long time to come.

I checked my e-mail every hour until the sweltering heat forced me to seek refuge in the shower.

Not the hottest summer on record, yet the interior of my apartment was still stifling. The third floor unit didn't rise above the surrounding structures and breezes were non-existent. If it weren't for the stunted trees growing out of tiny plots of soil at curbside, the only shade my building would enjoy were the shadows cast by the neighboring apartment complexes. I kept the single window closed because the metro buses passing through the neighborhood every fifty-five minutes released a noxious cloud of exhaust fumes that funneled directly up to my room. After almost asphyxiating during the first month, I finally shut the vapor trap of a window, and discovered the temperature hardly changed. Until winter. Once the cold weather arrived, freezing rain leached every vestige of heat from the entire building.

I emerged from the bathroom wrapped in a towel, my hair clipped high on the crown of my head. The message light blinked on my cell phone. Wet curls bounced as I darted across the space, creating a breeze with the speed of my passage. The text was from Stefano, an unfortunate one-time date I'd made the mistake of going out with on two occasions. He kept trying to rekindle the flame of romance in a fire gone dead. Not only were the ashes cold, the hearth had been swept clean. I'd been enthralled by his handsome features, and okay, his muscular thighs. He'd asked me to join him for coffee. He looked nice in a pair of tight jeans, so I'd agreed. Things progressed well, so long as he didn't talk. Problem was, he never stopped.

I declined his invitation for cocktails and turned the sound off on my phone. It was barely seven in the evening but I ate leftovers and crawled into bed with a book, bemoaning how my life had taken a sharp downward turn.

CHAPTER THREE

On Friday morning, I found an e-mail waiting in my mailbox with a return address I recognized. My excitement mounted as I clicked on the link and read what Professor Baumgarten had written.

Meet me at the south corner of campus on Saturday at 8am. You're my new apprentice. I can offer you

5% of my commission – which will probably be as pitiful as it sounds. We'll discuss details on the way. You should consider this opportunity the perfect solution for your useless college education.

I squealed through a mouthful of biscotti, spraying crumbs all over the keyboard. Disregarding the smirking tone of the message, I had only props for the professor. She cut directly to the heart of the matter and offered me a job.

I spent the day taking care of household chores and collecting the few items the Professor had suggested I bring along. I reread her message and wondered what I'd be doing the next day. Internet research clarified that estate appraising involved assessing and identifying items of value, a process I could imagine by mentally sorting through my parents' house.

Campus was deserted when I arrived at the corner and took up my post fifteen minutes early. I sipped my coffee and wondered what sort of vehicle my new boss drove. At exactly eight o'clock an older model Suburban careened around the corner and shuddered to a halt at the curb. The faded green paint was scratched, the fenders marked by rust, and the wheel-wells caked with mud. Professor Baumgarten waved from behind the wheel.

I climbed inside. She wheeled into traffic before I figured out where to stow my cup so I could snap on the seatbelt. Discovering the lack of a shoulder strap, I resorted to holding the coffee between my jean-clad knees and cinching down the straps of the lap belt. By the time I was secured to the worn bench seat, the truck had streamed back into traffic, just another member of the herd.

Professor Baumgarten reached over, grabbed my available hand, and shook. "Glad you contacted me, Lydia. You specialized in modern art, right?" She didn't wait for a response. "You're perfect for this job."

I made a sound of agreement, for what it was worth, considering that her constant stream of words reminded me of a rushing water tap. I remembered how you had to wait for a gurgle in the pressure to squeeze in a response.

"Well that's excellent, although mostly worthless in the modern job economy, as I'm sure you've discovered. To make it in this industry, you have to find a niche. I'm happy to share my success, because there's more than I can handle alone. Besides, the only way you get into this business is by being mentored." She stopped talking long enough to threaten a guy in a red BMW with a clenched fist while she changed lanes.

I seized the miniscule pause and jumped into the conversation. "Where are we going? What will I be doing?" I made a grab for the door handle when the suburban swerved into the exit lane and shot down the off-ramp toward another freeway access. We were headed out to the suburbs.

The vantage point of the tall vehicle was cool. I enjoyed looking down inside the cars we passed. For a woman of such small stature, the Professor handled the full-size truck like a professional obstacle course driver. The engine roared as she accelerated around a slow-moving van on the right, as if punctuating my admiration. I seldom drove. A car in the city was yet one more expense I couldn't afford. My old Honda sat abandoned at home, taking up valuable floor space in Dad's garage.

I realized silence had filled the interior and turned to glance at the professor. She glared at me, wearing the familiar pinched look that indicated she knew I wasn't paying attention. I offered a guilty smile of acknowledgement.

"As I was saying, you're about to get a crash course in estate processing. I usually start new assistants on small projects, but today we're on our way to Melbourne House." She waited for my reaction, but as soon as she realized my failure to be impressed, she pursed her lips and sent me a sour expression.

I shook my head and made an I-don't-know-that-name shrug. Pacified by my ignorance she began to lecture. This time I listened.

"Melbourne was the summer retreat of Machiavelli Montrose. He was a notorious playboy, a youthful libertine who held outrageous parties to which anyone who was someone was invited."

"Sounds like he knew how to throw a party."

She nodded emphatically. "His weekend gatherings created such a ruckus that the locals gave up the attempt to corral the drunk drivers and simply blocked the road after the party was in full swing. The blockade was not removed until the mass exodus occurred on Sunday afternoons. After one spectacular orgy of a weekend, that's a direct quote from *The Times*, in case you were wondering, the soirées came to an end. Machiavelli boarded a flight to Italy the next day and never returned."

"An abrupt exit for a guy having the time of his life."

Professor Baumgarten poked her finger in the air. "Bingo. Only hours later, a concerned relative contacted the police to make an inquiry about a missing woman. She was last known to have visited Melbourne House during the previous days. The next morning, a member of the local constabulary was sent out to nose around and found her body in the woods behind the house. She'd been dead approximately two days."

Fascinated, I listened with one hand braced on the dash and my coffee cup in the other. "What happened?"

The professor grinned. "Nothing, really. The death was written off as the result of alcohol intoxication, which seemed reasonable given the history of the place. In his defense, Machiavelli already had the plane ticket before the unfortunate incident occurred, having planned a lengthy visit to the Italian countryside."

"Convenient. Maybe too much so?"

"Suspicious little thing, aren't you?" She glanced sideways at me as she accelerated out of a turn. "I like that. Machiavelli's visit turned into a permanent relocation, and after the coroner changed his mind and decided the victim had died as a result of suffocation, things got interesting."

I was enthralled by the story, no longer paying attention to our route.

"News records indicate the U.S. threatened to extradite Machiavelli but nothing came of the posturing. By all accounts, the man became a model Italian citizen. He married the daughter of an impoverished aristocrat with friends in high places and duly produced the requisite batch of children. No one was ever formally charged in the death of Cara Lambert."

I tried to calculate how old the dead girl would be now.

"Machiavelli succumbed to age and infidelity last year." She chuckled at my curious expression. "He expired in the arms of his mistress, quite the scoundrel until the end. The beneficiaries just finished wrangling over the details in the will and I won the commission to process Melbourne House."

The unmistakable note of triumph in her voice was infectious. I responded with a touch of anticipation. "What sort of stuff do you expect to find?"

Professor Baumgarten beamed at me. "Wonderful things. Machiavelli Montrose was an avid art collector and he hobnobbed with the hot New York crowd at the time."

I opened my mouth but no sound came out. A list of artist's names from the 1960s streamed through my memory. A squeak finally squeezed out from my frozen vocal chords and emerged as a chirp that sounded like a cricket. A happy one.

The professor's lips stretched so wide, her coral colored lipstick smeared off on her incisors.

I understood her excitement now. The possibilities made me wriggle on the seat. I might rediscover the original work of an artist whose talent had filled my textbooks, possibly even graced the walls of major museums. I flexed my fingers around the paper cup from St. Pete's Coffee Hut and tried to expel my burst of nervous energy. The house had sat unoccupied for decades. I worried there might be little of value left inside.

Concern echoed in my voice. "What are the odds nothing has been stolen?"

Professor Baumgarten exhaled through clenched teeth. "That's always a possibility. In this case though, the word estate aptly describes the property's four acres of woods. There's even frontage to the adjoining lake which created an ongoing scandal during skinny-dipping weather. The neighborhood is built up with homes owned by the wealthy and somewhat famous. The houses are not the gigantic mansions found in the Adirondacks, but they aren't the typical weekend get-away cabins my family rented for summer vacation. Melbourne House boasts six bedrooms and all the usual comforts but hasn't been occupied in decades. We'll make a preliminary assessment about actually staying onsite during the inventory."

I thanked Professor Baumgarten for this opportunity.

She responded with a scoffing snort of sound. "You'll work your ass off, and when you get paid, you'll either grumble about how this was a huge waste of time or you'll think I gave you one of the best experiences of your life."

I leaned back against the seat and listened intently as she began to describe the steps involved in processing an estate. My enthusiasm not one bit subdued, I paid closer attention during the next ninety minutes than I had in any class I'd sat through in five years of college.

CHAPTER FOUR

Melbourne House

The visual was right out of a classic B movie. The house squatted at the end of a long drive, surrounded by thick stands of trees. The maple, beech, and birch foliage creating a kaleidoscope of greenery as a backdrop. The windows sat dark. I wondered if they were too dirty to reflect the weak sunlight or shuttered for security. Nothing appeared amiss as we drove closer, but if a monstrous figure shambled around the corner of the structure or a banshee started wailing from an upper window, I wouldn't have been surprised. I'd spent my PG13 years watching movies featuring houses just like this one. I knew nothing good ever came of going inside.

The setting was equally cinematic. Overgrown trees and shrubs flanked the drive, draping over the roofline like leafy shrouds. Despite the general air of neglect, the house itself looked to be in decent shape. No curtains fluttered through broken windows. No screens hung askew. No crooked shingles flaked off the steep rooflines. The paint had long ago crackled on the trim, producing an aged effect.

Professor Baumgarten shoved the gearshift into park and turned off the engine. She studied the exterior intently, her gaze taking in every detail. I split my attention between trying to figure out what she was searching for and watching her face in case she gave away a clue.

"Did you bring a clipboard?" She pulled her satchel from the rear floorboard and opened her door, hopping down with the energy of a woman half her age.

I grabbed my bag. I'd brought everything she'd listed at the bottom of her e-mail. Wanting to demonstrate my preparation, I scrambled out of the passenger side and caught up with her at the front of the vehicle. I brandished my clipboard. I'd stuck some paper under the clip. Clever me. College graduate.

The professor didn't even turn to look at me. She pointed at the exterior of the house and started talking. "The first thing you do is look for evidence of intrusion, primarily because you don't want to discover a group of transients living upstairs after you're already inside. I circle the structure and check for fractured windows or busted doors before entering. In old places like these, be extra cautious of cellars and basements. This house doesn't have a subterranean level, so no creepy dark underground exploration for you today."

"Wahoo," I said with enthusiasm; the lonely setting was already disconcerting enough.

The professor smiled briefly at my comment and continued speaking. "A caretaker comes by on a regular schedule, but I always err on the side of caution. If you have any doubts, sense a risk, get wobbly knees, or experience anything out of the ordinary, trust your gut and skedaddle. Never work in an unsafe place. If it's sketchy, take a friend. I've hired plenty of brawny students to hump furniture and flex muscles when I've worked in less savory neighborhoods. Squatters will move in if a property isn't monitored. Out here that's not the main problem. The estate contracts with a security firm and someone prowls the interior every week. They last visited two days ago, so I'm not too concerned."

I studied the secluded surroundings and then swiveled back around. "I'm surprised the windows aren't boarded up."

"Guess it's easier to fool strangers into thinking someone might turn up at any moment if the house is accessible."

As we circled the structure, I jotted down more notes.

The professor indicated an exterior light fixture. "There's a potential date-marker, the design is period to the architecture and provides a clue that the original features of the house may be intact." She tipped her head back and jabbed a finger skyward. "See that series of small stained glass windows up high along the third story? Those dormers belong to the attic space. Search 'em carefully. Attics are usually storage areas rather than living quarters. Good stuff gets squirreled away. Items of intrinsic value are almost always hidden. Families are often unaware the deceased relative possessed anything of worth. Then there are those that believe the reverse, insisting everything is priceless."

The only outbuilding was an open-wall parking structure, large enough to provide cover for half a dozen vehicles. I stood in the gravel pad at the rear of the drive and tried not to imagine people peeking at me from inside. The place was creepy but only because the location was remote. The nearest house might be just out of sight or a mile away. We had driven almost two hours to reach our destination and would spend a like amount going home. With half our work day eaten up in travel time, I half-expected we would stay over to finish the inventory. Sleeping in the house made a lot of sense but I had no enthusiasm for the idea. I really didn't want to stay here after dark.

My thoughts sparked a question. "Do you come to places like this by yourself?"

Professor Baumgarten shook her head. "My husband was going to tag along today, but after I made arrangements with you, he begged off. We drove out here last month to look around so I already had an idea of the distance. The security firm confirmed the utilities are working."

Circling back to the front, we climbed the steps to the porch.

"It's almost cozy isn't it?" I said, absorbing details of the exterior. When Professor Baumgarten didn't respond I turned to look at her.

She was staring at me. "Why do you say that?"

I shrugged. "Not what I was expecting, I guess. I figured the house would feel more abandoned."

The corners of Professor Baumgarten's mouth twitched. By the time I finished my inept explanation her grin stretched ear-to-ear.

"I think you have a sense for atmosphere, Lydia. Let's go inside. The first thing I do is complete a leisurely walk-through. I want to know what is present and get a general idea of where everything is located. I don't start an inventory until I've got a good grasp of the overall scale of the job."

"But you've been inside before, right?" I stepped closer as she pulled out a key and fiddled with the lock on the massive front door.

"I've only seen the main room downstairs. We're going to inspect the entire place today. I have no idea how much stuff may be inside. Since the house wasn't a full-time residence, I imagine it won't have the accumulated debris you find in homes occupied for decades." She rolled her eyes and grimaced. "Wait until you have to sort through the mountain of garbage saved during fifty years of marriage. This industry converts you into one of those people who recycle and donate on a regular basis."

Once inside, I could see that the rooms were sparsely furnished. On the first level we walked through the kitchen and pantry, peering in closets and opening cabinets. On the laundry porch we noted a built-in bureau. The drawers contained the sort of flotsam that accumulated over time, but I saw nothing to stimulate real excitement.

Professor Baumgarten made a lot of notations on her clipboard and kept up a running commentary about the relative market value of collectible items. I had no idea vintage tea tins were so valuable. The dining room held the expected furniture and bare walls. The table, with its mid-century lines and twelve matching chairs, caused my blood pressure to leap.

"That set looks very Eames-ish," I said, trying to keep my voice steady. The name referred to the well-known design duo from the 1950s.

Flipping over one of the chairs, professor Baumgarten pointed to the paper label still adhering to the bottom of the seat. "Good identification, Lydia. The complete set is a nice find. The timing is right for the pieces to be part of an original-run series, rather than a later reproduction line, but the Eames brand made a ton of stuff. Be sure to take close-up pictures of any labels or maker's marks you find." She eyed me speculatively. "How much do you think this would bring at auction?"

I calculated madly. I knew the single lounge chairs with their matching ottomans were all the rage in retro salons around the city. The modern knock-offs sold for hundreds of dollars. An original chair might pull close to three grand. A set of this size, in such excellent condition, had to be worth a lot more. "I'd guess at least twice as much as a matched pair of loungers."

Professor Baumgarten laughed. "Auctions are notoriously unpredictable. A table and chairs this large will take a special buyer, but the right person might pay a small fortune. If we advertise smart, we'll easily pull twenty grand, maybe more. Corporations spend big money to make the perfect impression in their conference rooms."

I tried hard to hide my shock.

"Your five percent would run about three hundred and fifty dollars." She winked at me.

Nice pocket change for a table and chairs I didn't even own. All I had to do was walk around and identify stuff and I profited. This had to be the best racket ever! My enthusiasm ratcheted higher. As we progressed, I learned about china, decorative ceramics, and American pottery ware. The sparsely furnished house now seemed to hold an endless supply of potentially valuable items.

The living room featured couches and other furniture pieces which had not stood the test of time. Stuffing had erupted from the arms of the camelback sofa and spilled into a yellowed cone on the hardwood floor. The silk upholstery on a matched pair of salmon-colored chairs had shattered into long strips, the fabric dangling over the exposed underlayment of coarse hemp. Mixed in among the seating arrangements were small tables, but it was the one positioned in front of the yellow couch that produced a squeal of glee from me.

I pointed an accusatory finger. "That kidney-shaped table might be a Noguchi."

Professor Baumgarten trotted over and inspected the glass top, leaning down close to peer at the base. She nodded her head. "I think you're right. The darn things are everywhere. The legs on this one are birch wood. If you ever find one with a cherry finish, do a happy dance and then package carefully because it'll be worth bucks. Unfortunately, this one will top out at about a grand." She made a notation on her clipboard.

That's all? Someday in the future, I wanted to be able to dismiss the value of an Isamu Noguchi coffee table. I wrote the name down along with her instructions to photograph from different angles. I had already filled several pages with notes.

Next, Professor Baumgarten walked over to study a bookcase jammed with objects. Magazines leaned drunkenly against a metal bucket filled with fist-sized rocks, slumping over and spilling out to cover the bottom shelf. I recognized the red trim and oversized covers of vintage issues of *Life Magazine* as well as the dull yellow spines of *National Geographic*. Thanks to my dad's interest in geology I identified the stones as probable geodes, likely from a local source. A stack of newspapers, the pages turned golden amber with age, sat on the hearth to the left of the stone-fronted fireplace.

Picking up an issue of *The New York Times* from fifty years ago, she displayed the cover and continued my on-the-job education. "Most houses don't have this kind of stuff. This place is unique because it's been sitting static all this time."

I pointed at the trio of paintings above the long couch. "I don't recognize the artist who painted these, but I feel like I should."

The watercolors were the typical compositions of sea and sand popularized on the Eastern Seaboard. I copied down the signature so I could search for the artist's identity in the databases compiled on the internet.

The professor dropped the newspaper back on the pile and slapped her palms together. "Let's check the upstairs."

The five foot wide staircase made a right-angled turn at a landing before continuing up to the second floor. I followed the professor, pausing near the top to look around. In the sitting area to the left, a quadrant of green wicker chairs circled a low table. The air up here felt warmer and drier to me, the result of natural heat induction, I supposed. The surrounding walls featured a number of closed doors.

The professor pointed to the right. "I've studied the floorplan and the master suite is that way. The bedroom has an attached sunroom, private bath, and his-and-hers closets." She indicated a pair of doors directly across from the top of the stairs. "Those are a set of matching bedrooms with an interior connecting door."

I tracked the motion of her hand as she continued down the row of five-panel doors.

"Next is the single bedroom in the corner, followed by another pair of linked bedrooms, and then the bathroom. That final door should be the stairway to the attic."

Next to the attic entrance was a window, almost as large as a doorway in scale, but obviously intended to offer passage to the outside. "Where does that go?"

"Access to the balcony. Rumor claims the dead girl was strangled inside the house, dropped off the edge, and her body discarded in the woods."

I imagined the scene. My overactive imagination supplied visceral details of the girl plunging to the ground. The resulting crunch of her inert form striking against the gravel produced a sympathetic shudder.

"How would anyone know that's what happened?"

The level of detail seemed implausible to me, considering no one had been arrested or charged with her death. If the cops knew so much, somebody must have information about the night she went missing. From outside, I'd seen the narrow balcony stretching down one side of the house. I thought the ledge was high enough up that the impact would have broken bones.

"Was the incident considered a homicide?"

Professor Baumgarten shook her head. "The official cause of death was listed as asphyxiation, but termed suspicious. And you're right, no arrests were made. Makes you wonder what else they knew, doesn't it?"

"And why they didn't, or couldn't, act on that information," I said, following her into the master bedroom.

My first sight of the enormous bed and matching dresser brought a twinge of distress. The bland design didn't appeal to me. I had a hard time envisioning anyone wanting the stuff, but the professor assured me there was a thriving market for such vintage pieces. The suite took less than five minutes for us to search, as the rooms were almost barren.

"The furniture looks like polished plywood."

She laughed at the note of complaint in my voice. "It probably is, you know how pop art influenced furniture design back in the 1960s. The blonde wood is more modern than the age of the house, but should still bring a reasonable price. I'm not surprised this bedroom is empty. The most personal items are found in bedrooms and those would have been retrieved." Professor Baumgarten's voice carried behind her as she exited the room and returned to the hall.

We worked our way down the row of doors, canvassing each bedroom. I found myself unwilling to venture off alone and explore like I had downstairs. My presence felt intrusive, an emotional reaction I hadn't experienced earlier, maybe because these rooms had been more private spaces rather than public. The whole thing made me feel voyeuristic.

The furnishings dated to the 1930s. The pieces were nicely constructed and with some cleaning and polishing would be very appealing. The double beds were crafted of walnut with matching burled inlay panels on the dresser drawers. Fine examples of the era, each set might fetch a fair price from dealers. The oversized round vanity mirrors of both dressing stations remained clear, the silvering not gone spotty or grown rotten with the passing of years. Once upon a time, the rooms had probably been luxurious but the lack of mattresses on the bare bedframes left a disconcerting sense of abandonment. Every closet was empty.

"What a disappointment!" Professor Baumgarten exclaimed as she closed the door of the third bedroom. "The furniture is in excellent condition but the style isn't as popular now. A decade ago they would have been worth twice as much. We'll be lucky to get five hundred dollars for each set." She slapped her clipboard against one thigh. "Based on what we've seen so far, this won't be a time-consuming job."

I followed her again as we approached the bedrooms at the far end of the second level.

The corner room featured an interesting trio of twin-size beds lined up along one wall, with a series of windows opposite. The space was large and the view was pretty. In the distance, I could see lake water sparkling between the trees. I was admiring the light and the view, thinking what a great art studio this space would make, when the professor called to me.

"Lydia, come take a look at this."

The odd tone in her voice made me hurry over. She was staring at the floor in front of the closed closet door. I peered around her side and saw a single word gouged into the hardwood plank, the name Cara. The carving was old. The wood had weathered and aged along with the rest of the interior.

A flicker of disquiet shivered through me.

"Cara Lambert was the name of the girl who died." Professor Bamgarten reached out and turned the handle on the closet, yanking the door wide. It was empty like the others. She tapped one foot on the floor. "Let's check the remaining rooms and take a peek upstairs before we complete the walk-through." She walked out of the room.

I stood a moment longer, unable to pull my gaze from the letters until I'd traced the lines of each one, imagining how difficult it would have been to carve the curved lines with such depth. I turned to follow the Professor and was enveloped in a faint floral scent. I frowned. The smell was familiar. A quick glance showed each of the windows was tightly shuttered. Sunlight streamed through the streaked glass panes to throw rectangles of brightness across the floor. The smell of lilacs suddenly permeated the air, thick and cloying, like a heavy perfume. I scampered through the door with undue haste, the hair on the nape of my neck raised in alarm, self-conscious about my silly reaction. Spinning around in the hall, I looked back through the open door, but the room was unchanged. I shuddered in a deep breath but the flowery odor was absent.

I cursed softly under my breath and made a beeline to catch up with my boss. Imagination or not, that was a little more atmosphere than I wanted to experience.

The last bedrooms contained only essential furniture. I followed professor Baumgarten, listening to her comments and observing her technique. She liked to pause just inside the entrance and survey the room, a quick glance offering a sense of the scale and layout. In all of the guest quarters, a painting had hung on the wall above each headboard. The compositions on the second floor were similar to the watercolors I'd seen on the first level, except they displayed various woodland scenes rather than seaside imagery. Each one had been meticulously matted and framed. I noticed the artist's name was the same as those from downstairs and double-checked the scrawled signature against the copy I'd made in my notes, before moving on.

By modern standards, the size of the bathroom was palatial, but given how many bedrooms were on this floor, the interior accoutrements seemed inadequate to me. I suppose the separate bathtub and shower was lavish for the era in which it had been built, but I couldn't imagine the number of potential guests being accommodated by a single toilet. Just thinking about the line queuing up in the hallway gave me the urge to pee.

"Can I use the bathroom or do I have to go out in the woods?"

"You can do either, but since the septic has been maintained, I would pee in the house."

I made a face at her before retreating inside and closing the door. The seat was chilly and the gurgling sounds that came from the old plumbing after I flushed were ominous. The water from the tap was as cold as ice. I dried my hands by wiping them down the front of my jeans and hurried to rejoin the tour.

Professor Baumgarten waited by the final door, her shoulder leaned against the wall. She finished writing something in her notes before straightening. "Next, the attic." She slanted a look at me. "Did you watch that movie from last summer, the one about those young people disappearing inside an abandoned cabin in the woods?"

"Now, that's just mean," I complained.

She laughed and twisted the knob, exposing a narrow flight of stairs. Half a dozen steps led to a square landing and then turned and continued up, similar to the way the main staircase was designed. The treads looked clean enough. Like the rest of the interior, a layer of dust coated the horizontal surfaces. Only a thin trail of movement indicated where the security personnel had passed on their rounds through the house. The flip of a switch lit the bare light bulb. The burst of illumination shone from the ceiling above the landing.

"Why is everything creepier the higher up we go?" Comfortable on the ground floor, the second level seemed eerily quiet. Now, contemplating climbing to the third, my feet were actually leaden. I glanced over one shoulder, half anticipating the sight of something spooky, but nothing looked wrong.

Professor Baumgarten gave me a friendly smile. "I think it's the intrusive factor. Even though we have permission to be here, the stamp of approval comes from someone other than the owner. We're intruders." She paused for a moment as if searching for the correct words. "The more private the space, the less comfortable it is to poke around. You can wait down here if you'd like."

I considered and rejected the idea. "No. I'm committed. In for a penny, in for a pound, right? I don't even know what that means but my grandmother says it all the time."

"I'll go first, just in case something multi-armed and ugly waits in the dark." She plowed up the stairs.

"You weren't this funny in class," I called after her retreating form.

CHAPTER FIVE

Struck Dumb

My comment produced a hoot of laughter from my new boss. The sound soothed my nerves. My hesitation to ascend the attic stairs stemmed purely from my own imagination. Nothing in the house had set my heebie-jeebies jangling, but the power of suggestion is potent.

"Jackpot!" Professor Baumgarten shouted from the top step. She darted forward and disappeared from view.

I scrambled up the steps.

The topmost floor was one large open space. The tiny dormer windows let in minimal light but another switch lit a trio of bare bulbs. Dozens of boxes and old trunks filled the center of the room. A pile of furniture sat stacked against the far wall, the chairs upturned on a tabletop, the forest of legs bristling in the glare of the light. My eyes were immediately drawn to a cloth-covered block between two of the stained glass windows. I could see the bottom corners of several frames sticking out the gap on the side.

Professor Baumgarten stood in front of a handsome Arts & Crafts wardrobe, a type of free-standing closet I recognized from antiquing expeditions with my mom. She'd already pulled open the doors and exposed the interior. The musty smell of old newspaper filled my nostrils as I hurried forward. Every cubby was packed solid. No space was left unused. Boxes and cartons, even paper sacks, filled the interior. Objects were stacked in every crevice, as if items had been crammed in the open spaces between the containers. I stood speechless for a full minute, wondering what treasures might be wedged inside, buried amid all the debris.

My attention drawn back to the paintings, I walked over and pulled away the canvas cover from the top of an ornate gilt frame. The gilded wood surprised me. I expected something more modern and less garish. The sliver of exposed surface at the top of the canvas made me think of a soft blue sky. Probably a landscape, I thought, and the medium was likely oil paint. The attic environment wasn't overly warm but decades of exposure would desiccate canvas. Whatever I found might require restoration work.

"Can I separate these frames and take a look, Professor Baumgarten?" I raised my voice to carry the short distance, unable to drag my gaze away from the cache.

Her response sounded loud in the quiet space. "Sure, just leave us room to move around."

I heard a thump and a bang as she displaced something. Though curious about the contents of the cupboard, my fascination with the stack of paintings was too strong to be distracted. Clearing away the dusty covering, I counted half a dozen frames, maybe more. Using gentle movements, so as not to disperse puffs of dust into the air, I moved the coarse fabric off to one side. The dry heat had kept the humidity low, a saving grace for art constructed from degradable mediums. I turned the first frame around and instantly recognized the familiar image. My hands started to shake. The yellow and white atomic mushroom cloud glared in the incandescent light. The repeating pattern, three across and three down, carried my eye to the unmistakable signature in the corner. I must have made a squeak of sound because quick footsteps crossed the room toward me.

"What's wrong, Lydia?"

I heard the concern in her voice as she approached, but I was stooped over, setting the canvas carefully back on the floor, and failed to respond. When I moved aside her gasp was audible.

"Is that –" She didn't complete the question.

I tried to breathe but the muscles in my chest didn't seem to work. "Yes, it is," I finally pushed out. "But it's likely a copy or a fake."

"Could be," Professor Baumgarten said. "Probably is." She clapped her hands together and cackled with glee. "But if it's genuine, we're in fat city!"

I couldn't tear my eyes away from the repeating images. I'd never been an admirer of Andy Warhol, but if I'd just held an original piece of his work, then I was his best new fan-girl. I sucked in three shallow breaths and cautiously slipped the frame aside to expose the one behind. At first I thought the surface was covered in a dark wrapper that hid the subject matter, but then the truth struck me. I'd seen a painting very similar to this one in every art history book that included painters from the twentieth century. This canvas, larger than the Warhol, offered a surface almost entirely a chocolate brown color. Along the bottom edge appeared a one inch brilliant vermillion line bleeding into a thin strip of rich golden hue. I searched for a signature but it wasn't until the professor produced the tiny flashlight attached to her key-chain that we found one on a corner and discovered the painting was upside down.

Professor Baumgarten patted my shoulder. "Don't have a heart attack, Lydia."

I sucked in a shaky breath. "Barnett Newman was a color field painter. His works are huge, like the side-of-a-gallery-wall big. This must be a sample or something." I turned my head to look up at her. "If these are genuine pieces, you need someone more experienced than me. I don't have the ability to authenticate them and don't want to risk damaging anything."

Professor Baumgarten's face took on an amused expression. "Don't be silly, Lydia. We won't. I'll call the lawyers and they'll contact the museums. Negotiations will proceed while a conservator is sent out to confirm if these items have any potential value. In the meantime, we finish our assessment and deliver the preliminary report." She motioned at me to keep going through the remaining pieces.

I exhaled another shivery breath and moved aside the Newman canvas. The next one to be revealed was completely unfamiliar to me but followed in the same vein as the other modern examples. By the time I shifted four more paintings I had found my groove again. I'd convinced myself these were just copies of famous works, nevermind the timeframe fit perfectly. Pushing aside the factoids of information my brain kept offering up, I tried to concentrate on my task. My concentration proved useless. My memory insisted on considering the fact that both of the artists whose work I had recognized, also operated studios in New York during the 1960s when Machiavelli had been in residence. I found it impossible to disregard the truth that both artists had been contemporaries of the same wealthy patron. I pulled aside the final framed work to expose the landscape that had initially caught my eye. It turned out the canvas wasn't done in oil and it wasn't even a painting.

"It's a collage," Professor Baumgarten said. Her brow wrinkled with concentrated effort.

I studied the disjointed images too. The entire surface had been heavily shellacked with something like varnish that had darkened and made the composition difficult to see. On the floor in front of it, I perched on my knees, studying each detail. I knew the style but couldn't place the artist. There was no apparent signature.

"It's a Romare Bearden," Professor Baumgarten said and her quiet voice impressed me. "I saw a retrospective of his work several years ago." She whisked her cell phone out of her pocket and dialed a number.

I stared at the painting. I recognized the name. An African American artist, as celebrated as any star of the Harlem Renaissance, Bearden was considered a modern American master. Surrounded by what might be literally hundreds of thousands of dollars' worth of art, and worried about the oil on my hands and the dirt on the paintings, I was stunned by the fact the art had sat here untouched for decades. The place could have burned down and no one would have known about the loss.

Machiavelli Montrose had never sold the house or returned to the U.S., but I still couldn't fathom why such valuable works had not been recovered. So little effort would be required to have someone come inside and remove the objects, package and ship them to Italy. Maybe he'd been so stoned or drunk he didn't remember the art? Possible. According to the stories Professor Baumgarten had shared on the drive out this morning, his parties were notorious for the degree of hedonistic pleasure had by all.

We traipsed back down two flights of stairs and halted for a lunch break. Professor Baumgarten unpacked a cooler from the rear of the suburban and handed me a Ziploc bag filled with a thick deli-sliced turkey sandwich. She followed that with snack bags of fruits and vegetables. I snagged a bottle of sweetened coffee drink from the ice chest and twisted off the lid, gratefully drinking half of the beverage in a long draught. My jumpy nerves kept me imagining a series of irrational scenarios, each one ending with the house bursting into flames, until I forced my attention back to the professor.

"What happens now?"

She swallowed her bite before responding. "When you find objects of extreme value, the estate usually tries to re-negotiate the agreed-upon rate." She pointed her finger up toward the attic. "This situation is why you always need a signed contract which specifies a flat rate, as well as a percentage."

I nodded, absorbing the information. Dollar signs danced around my head. "What happens if the paintings *are* legit?"

She took another bite of her sandwich and chewed, her brows furrowed in concentration, until finally she swallowed. "Once authentication is confirmed, the people who are in charge of the dispensation of the estate will decide how to conclude the matter. Usually the objects are sold, either at auction or to a private bidder, and the end-price determines the amount of my commission. In a case like this one, with so many valuable pieces, I might re-negotiate for a reduced rate just to close out the deal and get paid. Some auctions don't meet expectations. Occasionally, families decide not to sell."

"What happens in that situation?" Anxiety bloomed in my gut. I desperately wanted the pieces to be legit. I longed to be able to claim I took part in this incredible find. Mostly I wanted to enjoy my cut of the proceeds. What can I say? I'm greedy.

Professor Baumgarten pursed her lips. "There isn't a polite way to put it, but if that's the case, then I get screwed. You get screwed by default. Nobody has an orgasm, and we all go home unhappy, except for the heirs. Generally speaking, they're usually pretty content."

The unexpected analogy brought a gurgle of laughter.

After lunch we got down to serious work. Professor Baumgarten gave me tasks on the first floor. She handed me a copy of the floorplan and told me to mark anything of interest for follow-up.

"Don't forget to search for hidden closets, cupboards, or storage spaces." She shouted down to me as she climbed the stairs.

I went to work.

As much as I wanted to explore more of the upstairs, working where daylight entered the windows was nice. I didn't have a lot to sort. I shifted the furniture around, searching for information to identify the maker. I knew from my mom's experience with hunting for antiques, that even ruined pieces can still have value, if the internal structure is sound. Reupholstering gets expensive but the end-result often proves worth the price. Despite a thorough search, I failed to find any distinctive identifiers on the couch or sofa. The coffee table already had a tentative identification and I tagged two side tables as possible Bauhaus style pieces – I just didn't know the identity of the designer.

After I located and photographed every visible label, I went back through the rooms, adding my personal thoughts to the information in my notes.

The sideboard in the dining room, a blocky uninspired design, produced an ornate logo branded into the wood surface of the back panel. The piece must have been made of solid maple or some equally hard wood, and weighed approximately a metric ton. I planned to scour the internet to identify if the monstrous furniture had any potential value.

I documented what I could. By the time I checked my watch at four o'clock, surprised by how quickly the hours had passed, Professor Baumgarten had descended from the upper levels with her phone clamped to one ear. From my vantage point in the living room, I watched her exit the house, talking into the receiver. A nosy peek out the front window showed her flipping through the files in the front seat of the suburban and satisfied my curiosity. She didn't appear happy or angry so I minded my own business and continued working.

I'd saved the worst for last. A small cupboard at the back of the laundry room offered a smattering of cleaning products in cans that had long ago rusted out, leaving behind a thick orange-colored sludge. Finding nothing of interest besides the vintage washing machine, I turned to the kitchen. The cupboards still contained food and the sight of the boxes and cans, tins and wrappers, affected me in a way the rest of the house had not. This room gave the impression of abandonment, whereas the others had simply looked neglected and in need of a good cleaning. I poked at a few items but anything permeable had been infiltrated by rodents. Desiccated droppings littered the shelves.

Thankfully, the refrigerator door had been removed somewhere along the way and lay propped against the pantry wall. I couldn't imagine what kind of biological hazard the interior had once contained and was grateful not to know. I squatted down and peered in the triangle of shadow behind the curved face of the door. Nothing. I pondered more on why no one had emptied the house. Obviously there had been a constant trickle of people monitoring the structure. After the passage of so many decades, maybe nobody remembered anything remained. The presence of the regular security patrols didn't negate my line of reasoning, because how many of them would recognize a Vermeer from an Oldenburg?

The crunch of tires on gravel raised the hair on the nape of my neck. Apparently, I wasn't as relaxed inside the old house as I thought. I darted over to the front window in time to see a blue sedan with a gold stripe painted down one side, pull up beside the suburban. The word security was emblazoned across the hood.

Professor Baumgarten approached the man who climbed out of the driver's seat, reaching out to shake his hand. I watched the passenger door open and a second man unfold his body to stand up. His physique was that of a body-builder but the compact firearm strapped to his hip said he didn't rely on muscly bulk alone. I admired the show for a moment before returning to my task. The presence of an onsite security detail calmed my nerves slightly.

Shortly thereafter, exhausted and filthy, we headed back to the city.

CHAPTER SIX

The Plan

Professor Baumgarten steered the big truck down the country lane as she outlined her plan for the next day. "I don't normally work on Sunday, but under the circumstances, we should be there early in the morning. Bring an overnight bag." Her gaze darted to my face and although I rearranged my features she saw my skepticism. "Don't worry. I won't make you sleep in the spooky house. I'll book us a room at the

Red Light Inn out on the interstate. It's only thirty minutes away."

I experienced a spasm of relief. My imagination happily worked overtime when provided with fertile atmosphere, but I still felt certain I hadn't imagined the flutter of lilac scent when I'd been upstairs. I forced my attention back to the present. "When will the stuff inside get removed?"

The Professor frowned. "I insisted the attorneys for the estate contact one of the security firms who contract with the local museums. The MOMA has offered storage space until authenticity is determined. Even if the paintings turn out to be copies, nobody wants to risk the possibility they aren't."

I'd learned during my internship at that same facility that not every piece of art made by a famous person has a high value. The public tends to fixate on the dollar price paid for art publicized at auction, but the remainder of an artist's body of work is generally valued at greatly reduced levels. Of the three pieces we thought we'd identified, each of the artists had multiple works displayed in museums all over the country. All names were synonymous with the development of the field of modern American art. I tuned back into Professor Baumgarten's words.

"Security will be onsite until the courier truck arrives Monday morning. I don't want to worry about someone deciding this is the weekend to break in and nose around. There's always the added concern that a rumor about a major art discovery will circulate and prompt someone to investigate." She glanced over and caught my blank expression. "People talk, Lydia. Word of our find is already on the wire."

I relaxed wearily on the springy seat, slightly disillusioned by the realization that even the museum professionals weren't above horning in on our action. Cracking the seal on the last bottle of iced coffee, I inhaled the chocolaty aroma and hoped Professor Baumgarten would stop on the way home and let me pee. "Have you ever found anything like this before?"

"Twice. The first one happened early in my career and involved a coin collection inside a hatbox on the top shelf of a closet. The second time occurred just last year." She flipped on the turn signal and maneuvered deftly around a slow-moving sedan. "I found an original Rembrandt in a tacky black wood frame, like the kind you buy at the dollar store. Not a big painting and not a major work, but an authentic Rembrandt nonetheless."

I made an appreciative noise around the cookie I'd stuffed in my mouth.

"I know, so weird, isn't it? Art travels unexpected distances. Information gets lost. The granddaughter insisted on having the estate appraised but relatives had gutted the contents before the lawyers ever got involved. I dragged the painting out of a pile of boxes earmarked for donation. Somehow that Rembrandt made its way across an ocean to hang on the wall of an insurance broker in Hoboken, New Jersey. I suspect he took it in trade, not knowing it had real value."

"Just another art treasure with no provenance," I said. She gave an answering nod. It happened more often than the public thought. Objects get disconnected from their stories. Every generation likes something different. Some people abhor the old stuff, others hate the new, and treasures are discarded and rediscovered on a regular basis.

"Thank you for this opportunity, Professor Baumgarten. I'm fascinated and excited, and still nauseous." I patted the clipboard jutting out the top of my bag and realized how much I'd learned in a few hours. "Today was amazing."

She laughed softly. "Trust me, when I say this situation is not typical. Machiavelli moved in exalted circles. I can't say I didn't expect something, but without the attic contents, I'd be disappointed by what we found."

The drive back to the city was uneventful. We stopped for gas and I darted inside the convenience store to use the restroom. Heavy dusk had already fallen when Professor Baumgarten dropped me in front of my apartment.

"I'll pick you up in the morning. Be outside and ready to go at eight."

I saluted and she drove away.

CHAPTER SEVEN

Removal Day

Enlisted by Professor Baumgarten, half the university foot-ball team reported for duty the next day. They arrived just before noon, erupting out of a mid-sized SUV, expressing the profound enthusiasm only pumped-up athletes can generate.

I was amused by the expression of alarm that crossed the face of the junior curator. Standing on opposite sides of the room, I studied him as his gaze followed the football players trampling up the porch steps to shower Professor Baumgarten with boisterous greetings. The man's two weedy curatorial assistants took shelter behind their superior, casting baleful glares over his narrow shoulders, as if they expected the football players to view them as the opposing team.

Under the disinterested regard of several serious-looking security personnel, the Professor shouted out instructions over the bedlam. Fueled by energy drinks, and with a precision rivaling that of a flock of Canadian geese, the new labor force thundered up the stairs to the second floor. The nervous museum representatives, grim security personnel, and the offensive line jumped the testosterone level in the house to a significant level.

Two security personnel were assigned to each floor, for what purpose, I had no idea. It seemed unlikely we'd need to fight off an armed attack over the Eames furniture or foil a premeditated attempt to abscond with the paintings.

I congratulated myself for having the foresight to pack caffeine this morning and poured myself a cup of coffee from the thermos. Then I set about organizing the color-coded packing labels.

The museum staff scuttled upstairs. I assumed they were anxious to breach the third floor and lay eyes on the real treasure. It didn't take much imagination to visualize the junior curator preparing to barricade the door to the attic stairs with his frail body as a dastardly linebacker attempted a snatch-and-grab for the Warhol. I amused myself playing out the scene with various conclusions while my own security detail observed my movements.

The security personnel could have been cloned from the body-builder I'd seen yesterday. It took me a while to realize they belonged to two different groups. The museum people had accompanied the firm the MOMA used to transport items of interest. The others were from the firm hired by the Montrose estate to monitor the house and contents. They might have been molded from a master copy, each replica oddly similar with an expression that never showed a hint of anything but polite disinterest. Despite my broad smiles and attempts at scintillating conversation, the men remained stoic and non-responsive.

It wasn't long before the football players began carrying furniture downstairs. I directed them to deposit bed frames and wicker chairs in the appointed staging areas. Muscles slid beneath the torn blue jeans and ratty t-shirts and made the task look effortless. The sight reminded me of the all-male review some girlfriends had coerced me into attending during my twenty-first birthday bash in Atlantic City. Good times.

As the rooms filled up, the boxes we'd filled with magazines and books earlier that morning had to be shifted aside to make more open space. The guys trotted up and down the staircase, barely a gleam of sweat appearing by the time the entire second floor had been cleared.

Professor Baumgarten called me upstairs to confirm everything had been collected. I trailed in her wake as she made a final search for hidden cupboards and missed objects, averting my eyes from Cara's name where it was carved into the floor behind the door of the corner bedroom.

"The attic will take longer because I'll need to pack as we clear the room. I want you to stay on the ground floor and direct traffic. Make sure everything gets deposited in the correct staging area according to the plan."

"When is the first truck scheduled to arrive?" I knew from the debriefing on the drive out that she had completed arrangements to have transport vehicles dispatched from various sales and auction outlets.

"Three are scheduled for this afternoon and two for tomorrow morning, plus the museum people will transport the paintings."

We both inadvertently raised our gaze up to the ceiling as if we could see through the layers of flooring to where the stacked canvases leaned drunkenly against the attic wall.

Professor Baumgarten recovered first. "I want everything downstairs, and the upstairs levels cleared, before anything officially leaves the premises. The truck-loading process is efficient when everything is properly pre-staged. Good organization also cuts down on the chances of something being sent to the wrong place."

We passed one of the security guards as we exited the master suite. He stood statue-straight, his arms hanging loose at his sides, prepared for immediate action.

I jerked my head toward him. "Is he expecting a crack team of thieves to swing through a bedroom window?"

Professor Baumgarten's response indicated similar amusement. "He's probably more concerned about the museum people attacking a member of the football team for sweating too close to the paintings."

I glanced toward the attic access where the curatorial staff hovered, waiting for permission to ascend, and tried to imagine the scene. The Professor had to tap the top of my clipboard to get my attention.

"I want you to go back downstairs, Lydia. Make sure the correct color of label gets attached to every box and piece of furniture. Cross-check the inventory sheet and write out a receipt for each destination. You want to make sure the numbers match our inventory sheet, the driver's receipt, and the label on the object."

We'd already reviewed this part several times but I appreciated the clarification. The last thing I wanted to do was screw up and be responsible for sending a delivery to the wrong destination.

I descended the stairs to the ground floor as Professor Baumgarten led the crowd to the attic. Somewhat disappointed I didn't get to witness the curatorial folks act like excited puppies, I celebrated our progress with chocolate.

I like to reward myself.

I perched on the hearth and ate a Butterfinger candy bar. My offer to share with the security guys was politely declined, much to my relief because I really didn't want to share. It is chocolate, after all.

I measured progress upstairs by what was brought down. A member of the football team relayed the curious information about how the junior curator and his assistants had formed a protective ring around the paintings while the space was cleared.

"Strange little guys, but they seem nice enough." He said as he deposited a plastic bin where I pointed.

I watched his denim-clad backside until it disappeared up the stairs and didn't blame the curatorial staff for being over-protective. Every brawny thigh that stomped past the stack of frames would have caused me to wince and bare my teeth too. I tortured myself by imagining the dust boiling up to obscure the delicate surfaces of the paintings.

Now I was extra grateful that Professor Baumgarten had permitted me to go back upstairs first thing in the morning and ogle each canvas for a moment. I enjoyed a glorious moment of self-satisfaction and then a disconcerting second or two of annoyance that finders-keepers didn't apply. Funny how seeing the real thing in an I-can-reach-out-and-touch-it kind of way made me desire something I had no real prior interest in owning. I guess that's how the regular guy goes down the primrose path and becomes an art thief.

The night security detail waited patiently until we departed before enacting the changing of the guard.

I recognized the contents of the wardrobe that had been emptied into the plastic totes the Professor had brought with her this morning. As each one was carried downstairs, I had them stacked against a bare dining room wall where they could be catalogued in greater detail.

The echo of voices carried downstairs for a while, but no further deliveries occurred. I found a place to perch and waited, counting off the minutes and trying to decipher the sounds of commotion above. Eventually a cry of success went up and a few moments later the wardrobe appeared in the stairwell.

It took a while to get all the details but I finally pieced together what had caused the delay. To the consternation of the movers, they found that while two men could heft the heavy wooden cabinet down the staircase, negotiating the sharp turn at the landing halted progress. After several aborted tries, experimentation discovered the single position that allowed the piece to angle through the narrow opening and progress continued.

By early afternoon I was a style wreck. My hair, which had started the day in an upswept bun, had escaped its confines to create a halo effect around my face. I could feel the grit of dust on my skin and looked forward to a hot shower. Professor Baumgarten's appearance was no different than when she'd arrived at my apartment just before eight that morning, even though she'd been up and down the two flights of stairs at least a dozen times. Clearly, I needed more exercise.

I created room in the kitchen for the surplus of tables and chairs we'd found in the attic and sent the football players outside to raid the cooler in the rear of the Professor's Suburban.

Once our business was finished in the attic, the museum people could get to work on the paintings. Presumably, the curator and his minions would securely crate each piece for transport under the watchful eyes of the security guards.

We halted for a late lunch, filing outside to enjoy the sunshine and fresh air.

Professor Baumgarten offered me a bottle of water and a Ziploc lunch bag. "So, what do you think of the estate business so far?"

I was stymied trying to put my thoughts into words. The exploration process was creepy but titillating. The sorting and packing of the estate, and organizing it for transport, was a labor-intensive process but I loved the detailed tracking. Mostly I loved the feeling of being able to use the knowledge I'd learned in school, and doing a job outside the normal expectation of nine to five had its own appeal. The freedom associated with not being in a confined office space was pretty wonderful too.

"I love it." I said without hesitation. "It's fascinating and exciting. I feel like a voyeur with a license to peep."

The Professor grinned back at me.

After lunch, I resumed my role as personal secretary and followed Professor Baumgarten around as she put the team back to work.

The muscle parade continued as the boys moved items and wrapped furniture in moving blankets.

Eventually, the time came to remove the paintings from the attic. The junior curator's chest puffed up like a bantam rooster in the presence of a rival. He sputtered out cautions as the paintings were carted down two flights of stairs, fluttering his arms the entire way. I could almost hear the feathers rustling when he bustled out the front door.

Once the crates were strapped inside the rear of a plain white Ford Econoline van, the museum staff clustered inside while the paperwork was finalized with Dr. Baumgarten. Two security guards climbed into the front of the van and another pair followed in an unmarked sedan. And then they were gone, carrying away the art I'd had a hand in recovering.

The sense of urgency died away after that.

I placed checkmarks beside each item on our detailed inventory as we worked our way through the ground floor rooms but our pace was slower. The meticulous records tracked the location of where each piece had been found, where it had been packed, and the destination where it would be auctioned or sold. The process of going through each room was methodical, a necessity given the volume of material that was being removed in a short time.

Ironically, the paintings had been the last items to be dealt with and the first to depart the premises. I wondered if Machiavelli Montrose, from his comfy chair in the ether, was aware that his long-lost treasures were about to be shared for the first time in decades.

The furniture was next on the list to be loaded and removed. As the Professor directed her team of porters, I con-

ducted an unofficial survey of the biceps bulging out of shirt-
sleeves and decided the guy in the navy blue t-shirt was the
winner. Hands down.

The household contents had been sorted into piles based
on final destination. Each object had to be appropriately
tagged with the correct color. Items with blue tags, which
included most of the furniture that appealed to specialty
dealers, was loaded into the huge moving van destined for an
auction house. The objects with yellow labels were headed to
a high-end resale boutique in Soho that specialized in mid-
century style and pop culture kitsch. Everything labeled with
the red identifiers would land at an antique collective that
specialized in collectors.

Professor Baumgarten controlled the flow of materials
out the door, taking responsibility for seeing that the right
things made it into the correct transport vehicle. She made it
look easy. I noticed she never deviated from the system.

I paid attention because her process worked. I could see
how bedlam would result if you didn't follow a plan. This industry would not appeal to a disorganized personality.

The Professor collected signatures and handed out re-
ceipts for every item loaded, checking everything in triplicate
before anyone departed.

By six o'clock that evening, the Machiavelli Montrose estate was nearly processed.

I was impressed with the speed events had taken, and also of how adept Professor Baumgarten was at delegating

tasks. I made a note of how a team of reliable personnel was invaluable and documentation, critical.

"That's about it for tonight." Dr. Baumgarten said as she watched the last piece of furniture being strapped inside the panel truck. She turned to look at me. "I've got another big project scheduled toward the end of the year. If the details pan out, I'm going to need someone to take over the smaller jobs while I'm busy, are you interested, Lydia?"

I straightened my posture, my spine stiffening like that of a soldier about to snap out a salute, although I managed to restrain myself. "Yes, Ma'am."

And that's how I became an estate appraiser.

CHAPTER EIGHT

The Good News

So, what happened? Well, mostly lots of good news. In the end, museum officials took almost six months to authenticate the pieces as legitimate works of the representative artists. Two additional paintings were attributed to moderately known modernists, and the others enjoyed a new cachet from being associated with such a treasure trove of modern art.

The event caused a minor ripple in the New York demimonde, especially after the collection was assessed.

Everything is relative.

I should be so lucky to own items of such paltry worth.
The heirs of the Montrose estate settled for an undisclosed
amount in a private deal with the Museum of Modern Art,
and the commission was duly paid.

Even Professor Baumgarten didn't know the exact price
tendered for each piece, but she could estimate based on her
cut of the proceeds.

The Eames dining set turned out to be absurdly rare and
sold at auction for $118K. The table and chairs now grace
the conference room of some Fortune 500 corporation. The
blocky sideboard proved to be a Danish original, from some
artist whose name I still cannot pronounce, and brought a
completely unexpected whopping $52K at auction. I almost
wet myself with excitement. From that moment on, I prom-
ised to embrace all objects, new and old, in the light of potential profit and restrain from making snap judgments based on
appearance alone. No matter how ugly I think they are.

The remaining furniture and household items produced
an additional $20K but the watercolors I'd admired on both
the lower and upper floors turned out to be worthless. Most
didn't even sell. The *Life Magazines* earned a tidy sum from a
collector in California, as did the canned products from the
kitchen pantry. Collectors are weird. No matter what you
find, somebody collects it. The hoarders of the world love
that idea.

One of the most interesting items came from the packed wardrobe in the attic, an unlined journal with the interior pages covered in written notes and doodles. Some of the scrawls bore a distinct resemblance to the signatures found on the works of world-renowned artists. Guests had obviously scribbled their names and penned ribald poems during the weekend festivities at Machiavelli's house.

I could imagine the object setting on the Noguchi table and being passed around the room during cocktails. I never saw the book but Professor Baumgarten showed me the pictures she'd taken of the interior. The lewd comments written beside several names left an unpleasant association in my mind.

Misogyny had been alive and well back in those days, the women's movement just gaining traction in the national eye. The name of the girl who'd been asphyxiated also appeared in the journal. Someone had drawn a thick black line through her signature, the slash of ink pressing hard enough into the surface of the page to leave an indentation. I couldn't help but wonder if she'd been one of those outspoken young women, raising her voice on behalf of her collective sisterhood. Might that have had anything to do with her being silenced?

An autograph collector's wet dream, the police confiscated the book with talk of reopening a cold case investigation, much to the consternation of Machiavelli Montrose's descendants.

I guess it's never too late to seek justice for the wronged.

Still, I wonder about the person who gouged Cara's name into the floorboard of that bedroom and question the motivation that drove someone to perform the act. Every time I dredge up the memory of those letters, recall the way the shapes were carved into the plank surface with such a determined hand, the image never fails to produce a shiver. As does the scent of lilacs.

Despite the local interest generated by our find, I'm doubtful the mystery will ever be solved. Cara's name is remembered, but unless the dead suddenly start speaking from the afterlife, I suspect the truth about her death will remain unknown.

ABOUT LESANN BERRY

Lesann writes about messed-up people and sinister events, saying her stories often feature paranormal or romantic elements because life is boring without spooky stuff and warm bodies. Crossing genre lines, she pens both contemporary and historical mysteries, romantic suspense, and even a little horror.

Visit WWW.LESANNBERRY.COM for new releases.